ANIMAL TALES FROM
LISTEN WITH MOTHER

ANIMAL TALES FROM
LISTEN
WITH MOTHER
With an introduction by
Jean Rogers

Illustrated by Douglas Hall

*Published in association
with the BBC*

HUTCHINSON
London Melbourne Sydney Auckland Johannesburg

Hutchinson Children's Books Ltd

An imprint of the Hutchinson Publishing Group
17–21 Conway Street, London W1P 6JD

Hutchinson Group (Australia) Pty Ltd
30–32 Cremorne Street, Richmond South, Victoria 3121
PO Box 151, Broadway, New South Wales 2007

Hutchinson Group (NZ) Ltd
32–34 View Road, PO Box 40-086, Glenfield, Auckland 10

Hutchinson Group (SA) (Pty) Ltd
PO Box 337, Bergvlei 2102, South Africa

First published 1984

Set in Baskerville by BookEns, Saffron Walden, Essex

Printed and bound in Great Britain
by Anchor Brendon Limited, Tiptree, Essex

ISBN 0 09 155260 5

The publishers would like to thank Valerie McCarthy
for her help in selecting the stories

Contents

Introduction

My children grew up with 'Listen with Mother'. At about the time I joined the programme in the early seventies, Jeremy, my eldest child, was two. He always enjoyed being read to. When he was only a year old he would sit on my lap and encourage me to make up stories about the pictures he saw in his nursery rhyme book.

When I started reading stories for 'Listen with Mother', I would invariably pretend I was in my dining room – not sitting in front of a microphone in the studio – and that I was telling the stories to Jeremy, and only to Jeremy. It is a very personal activity, story-telling, and I am sure it only comes across on radio if it is approached on a one to one basis. The dining room had a bright yellow floor and I'm certain that's why all my precious memories of the programme are bathed in sunshine!

Telling stories to children encourages their imaginations and their understanding and use of words. It certainly worked in Jeremy's case. By the time he went to 'big school', although he was still unable to read, his teacher – a lovely lady called Mrs Lowrie whom my son adored! – would sit him in front of the class where, she said, he would tell the other children the most wonderful stories all by himself.

It is such a special, magical experience cuddling a little one to you and sharing a good story such as the ones you will find in this book. Children especially like stories about animals. Tell them it's about a cat, or a tortoise, or a singing hippopotamus, and just see their eyes light up. I sometimes wish Justine, my youngest child, was not past the stage of sitting on my lap, but she is twelve now.

However, the television character I play at the moment, in a series set on a farm, runs the local playgroup, so I still get opportunities to tell exciting stories to little ones; stories like 'The Owl Who Didn't Give a Hoot' and 'Frizby's Royal Invitation' (I still have a soft spot for stories with princesses in them) and say those nostalgic words: 'Are you sitting comfortably?' You are? Well, I'll begin.

Jean Rogers

Green grobblop

Eugenie Summerfield

Are you sitting comfortably? Then I'll begin.

At first nobody knew what the green grobblop was or even where it came from. Ben found it on the doorstep one Monday morning. He came running in from the garden calling to his mother.

'Come and see! There's a funny green hairy thing out here. It's ever so small and ever so sad. Can I play with it?'

Ben's Mum, who was in the kitchen doing the washing, came to have a look.

'I don't know what it is,' she said, 'and it doesn't look very clean. I think I'd better give it a good wash before you play with it.'

She always washed everything on a Monday. So she washed it. She was going to peg it up to dry when she heard it say, 'Don't peg me up on the clothes line. A green grobblop like me should be put in a nice warm room.'

Ben's Mum was so surprised to hear the grobblop speak, she said, 'Oh, I'm sorry!' and asked, 'What did you say your name was?'

'I'm a green grobblop,' it said, and it did look so small and sad. Ben's Mum was a kind lady. She took it at once and put it on the curly cuddly rug in the sitting room.

'That's much better,' said the grobblop, nodding its small green head. 'Now I should like tea and chocolate biscuits and some bananas.'

'There is only one banana,' said Ben, who was looking forward to eating it for his tea.

'Well, that will have to do for now then,' sighed the grobblop, looking smaller and sadder than ever. 'But in future, I would like three for my tea.'

After he had eaten the banana, the grobblop had four helpings of biscuits. He was just drinking his fifth cup of tea when Ben's Dad came home from work.

'What's that?' asked Ben's Dad. When Ben

and his Mum told him, Ben's Dad had to agree that the grobblop did look small and sad.

'And it will need to be well looked after,' he said.

All the rest of the week the grobblop sat on the curly cuddly rug. Ben's Mum fed him and Ben played with him whenever he wanted. At the end of the week Ben's Mum said: 'I'm afraid I shall need some more money now that we have a grobblop to feed. It does eat rather a lot.'

'I can see that,' said Ben's Dad, and he looked worried. He wasn't at all sure that his boss would pay him more money just because he now had a green grobblop to feed.

'Perhaps,' he said, 'when the green grobblop gets bigger and stronger, he'll be able to do some useful jobs about the house.'

'I hope so,' agreed Ben's Mum. She had been doing everything for the grobblop, giving him the biggest helpings, letting him have the most comfortable place to sit in the sitting room and the warmest blankets on his bed.

'I can think of lots of useful things he could do,' said Ben's Mum.

No sooner was this said than the grobblop said, 'I'll have to go to bed. I'm not at all well.'

The doctor was called and he came almost at once. He wasn't used to treating grobblops, but he said, 'He does look green and small and sad!

He needs someone to look after him. He's to stay in bed a day or two and take this medicine to make him well and strong.'

The grobblop liked his medicine almost as much as he liked tea and biscuits and bananas. He liked staying in bed even better than he liked lying on the curly cuddly rug in the sitting room. So he stayed in bed and had all his meals brought up. All the time he was growing bigger and stronger, Ben's Mum grew thinner and more tired. Until one day, she said, 'I'm quite worn out.' Ben's Dad sent her to bed and called the doctor who said, 'You're to stay in bed a day or two and let someone look after you.'

The grobblop heard what the doctor said. He peeped in to see Ben's Mum. 'She does look so sad and small,' thought the grobblop who was now big and strong. He felt ashamed. He went downstairs at once.

He cleaned the kitchen, dusted the rooms, and made a delicious meal which he took up to her on a tray. He did this every day until Ben's Mum was well again. Then he said to her, 'I've come to say it's time I went away.'

'You don't have to go,' said Ben's Mum. 'You really can stay as long as you like.'

But the grobblop replied, 'No, I'm big enough and strong enough to look after myself now. I won't forget how well you looked after me and I'll write to you sometimes.'

Ben and his Mum and Dad were quite sorry to say goodbye to the grobblop. He went to live at the seaside and he did write to them. He sent them some lovely picture postcards and he's asked them all to come and stay with him for their next summer holiday.

The adventures of Young Hedgehog and Mole

Vera Rushbrooke

Are you sitting comfortably? Then I'll begin.

Young Hedgehog and Mole were sitting at the bottom of the oak tree in the hedge, chatting.

'I lead such a dull life!' said Young Hedgehog. 'It's the same old things every day! Get up, have something to eat, sit in the sun, have something else to eat, have a chat with Rabbit, go to bed, and that's all I ever do! I wish I had a more exciting life!'

'I never thought about it before,' said Mole, 'but now you come to mention it, I suppose it is

14

rather dull doing the same old things every day.'

'Well,' said Young Hedgehog, 'should we change it by going out to find adventures?'

Mole thought a bit.

'Very well,' he said, 'but not for long as I've just started on a new tunnel.'

So they shut their little doors and set off to find adventures.

'This is exciting!' said Young Hedgehog, trotting along. 'We'll go a new way neither of us has been before.' So they trotted along the strange path, laughing and whistling. Presently they came to what looked like a tunnel.

'This looks interesting!' said Young Hedgehog. 'Should we go down this tunnel and see what's at the other end?'

'Well,' said Mole, 'I'm always going down tunnels! But this one is so big!'

So they crept into the tunnel.

'It's very dark!' said Young Hedgehog.

'Tunnels always are!' said Mole.

Just then, ahead of them, came a swishing, sloshing and splashing of water. And before they could say, 'Dandelions!' down the tunnel came a stream of water and it washed Young Hedgehog and Mole out of the tunnel and into the daisy field. For it wasn't really a tunnel they'd gone into, but a water pipe coming from the farm and somebody had turned on the tap.

'Goodness me!' cried Mole, 'I wasn't expecting that!' and he shook the water off his velvet coat.

'Never mind,' said Young Hedgehog, pretending he didn't care about getting soaked with water. 'That's part of the fun, isn't it?'

'Is it?' said Mole.

Then Young Hedgehog laughed and then Mole laughed, and they told each other it was fun having adventures.

After they'd dried themselves they trotted on, picking up a tasty bit here and there to eat on the way. After a while, they came across a big old basket full of cabbage leaves. There was a hole in one side of it.

'Let's climb in there,' said Young Hedgehog, 'and see what's inside.'

'Isn't it exciting doing new things!' said Mole. 'It's quite a change from digging tunnels!'

Just as they had climbed inside, the basket began to move. Someone was carrying it. Young Hedgehog and Mole were not sure what to do.

'We're moving!' cried Mole.

'Yes,' said Young Hedgehog, 'I wonder where we are going!'

'I don't think I like it very much,' said Mole. 'I like to know where I'm going to.'

'Oh, but that's the fun of it!' said Young

Hedgehog. 'It's not an adventure if you know where you're going.'

'I suppose not,' said Mole.

'Then look happy!' Young Hedgehog said.

Just as he said that, the basket of cabbage leaves with Mole and Young Hedgehog was tipped out into a chicken run. When the hens saw Young Hedgehog and Mole in their chicken run there was a great squawking and cackling.

'Out! Out!' shrieked the hens. 'Hedgehogs and rats are not allowed in here!'

Mole was furious.

'I'm not a rat! I'm a mole!'

'Whatever you are, you're not allowed in here. Just hens and chickens. Out with you!'

Young Hedgehog and Mole squeezed under the wire as fast as they could and trotted off.

'It was really fun, wasn't it!' said Young Hedgehog.

'No!' cried Mole. 'It wasn't! And I want to go home! I've been soaked with water in a tunnel, chased by angry hens, and I've been called a rat! I've had enough, I'm going home!'

'All right,' said Young Hedgehog, who was really glad because he wanted to go home too. So off they went.

When they got home, Mole said, 'Thank goodness! Let me get inside and have a warm sleep!' And he dived down his tunnel and nobody saw him for days.

Young Hedgehog, feeling cold and tired, opened his little green door and banged it behind him.

'From now on I'm going to stay at home! There's nothing nicer than doing the ordinary things you do every day like sitting in the sun, and eating something nice, and chatting with Rabbit, and having a nice warm sleep.'

And from then on, nobody ever heard Young Hedgehog talking about adventures.

Little Pig and the hot dry summer

Margaret Gore

Are you sitting comfortably? Then I'll begin.

'I wish it would rain!' said Little Pig.

There had been no rain for weeks and weeks, and all the pigs were puffing and grunting with the heat. In the field beyond the pigsties the ground was as hard as an overbaked cake.

No rain meant that there was no mud. And what Little Pig loved most of all was mud. Thick, squelchy, oozy *mud*! Little Pig would roll on his back, waving his four pink trotters in the air and squealing with delight.

'If *only* it would rain!' sighed Little Pig. 'This

19

summer has been so hot and dry, and I *do* love a mucky roll in the mud!'

In the sty next door to Little Pig lived Big Pig. Big Pig was a terrible boaster.

'*I* could make it rain – if I *wanted* to, that is,' he said. None of the other pigs believed Big Pig. Especially Quick Pig, who had a sharp tongue.

Quick Pig said, 'Go on then, *make* it rain, Big Pig!'

'I – I don't think I have time just now,' replied Big Pig.

Slow Pig grunted, 'He knows he can't, that's why.'

Big Pig pretended to be busy rooting about for something to eat. Slow Pig had hardly moved all summer – except to eat. He just lay by the wall, snoring. Even Kind Pig, who was a most patient pig, grew tired of Slow Pig's snoring.

The weather grew hotter and hotter. And *still* no rain.

'I don't think I shall ever have a good, mucky roll in the mud again!' wept Little Pig.

'Of course you will, Little Pig,' said Kind Pig. 'I'm sure it must rain soon!'

And it *did* rain. That very night.

First came a few big spots. Splash, splash, splodge. Then it rained faster and faster, and heavier and heavier.

Now it was simply bucketing down! The rain

hissed on the roof; it swept across the yard; it gushed down the drains.

It made a noise like a hundred pigs all drinking at once from a high trough!

But the trouble was, now that the rain had started it wouldn't stop. It went on all the next day, and all the next night, and all the next day after that!

'It's never going to stop raining!' squealed Little Pig. Quick Pig blamed Big Pig.

'*You* made it rain – and now you can't stop it!'

'It's not *my* fault,' grumbled Big Pig.

There was water everywhere. Even the field became a lake. The ducks from the pond were able to swim right up to the wall of the pigsties. *Inside*, the pigs were huddled together, squealing; and *outside* the ducks swam up and down teasing them, and laughing their quacky laughs.

The water got higher and higher. Little Pig was frightened, but Kind Pig said, 'Don't cry, Little Pig. Look, here is someone coming to save us.'

It was Tom the farmhand. He came sailing across the field on a wooden raft which he had just knocked together from an old door.

Tom put down a plank from the pigsties on to the raft, and then the pigs walked across it. First Quick Pig – because he was always first with everything (especially eating!).

Then Big Pig, because he had knocked every-one else out of the way. Then Kind Pig, who showed Little Pig how to walk along the plank without falling off, and lastly Slow Pig – it *had* to be Slow Pig didn't it!

The pigs sailed away on their raft, to a dry place on the other side of the field. And there they had to stay, until, next morning, they were awakened by Little Pig squealing and squealing.

'Wake up, wake up,' cried Little Pig. 'The sun's shining, and all the water has gone! We can go home.'

Little Pig was quite right. They did go home, but not by raft, because there was no water left. They had to go by tractor, because the whole field was a mass of – MUD!

'Squelchy, oozy, delicious MUD!' cried Little Pig. When they reached home, the pigs trotted happily back into their own sties. First Quick Pig, then Big Pig, then Kind Pig, and last of all, Slow Pig.

But where was *Little* Pig?

The pigs crowded to the wall and looked over into the field.

There was Little Pig. He was lying on his back in the mud, waving his four.pink trotters in the air and squealing with delight.

'I *do* love a good mucky roll!' said Little Pig.

The owl who didn't give a hoot

Irene Holness

Are you sitting comfortably? Then I'll begin.

'Tu whit tu whoo!' hooted Mrs Owl. 'Come, children. Now you-oo!'

'Tu whit tu whoo!' chorused three of the little owls perched on a high branch of the old oak tree.

'Itty ooo!' chirruped the smallest owl. His brother and his sisters chuckled.

Mrs Owl didn't think it was at all funny. She looked sadly at the smallest owl.

'Oh, Drew,' she sighed. 'Why can't you learn to hoot properly like Hugh, Sue and Pru?'

Drew looked up at the bright silver moon and tried again.

'Itty ooo, itty ooo,' he sang. 'I'll never get it right!'

All that night Drew practised hooting, but still all he could manage was 'Itty ooo,' in a funny, squeaky voice. At last, as the sun rose, the deep blue night sky began to grow lighter.

'Bedtime, children,' Mrs Owl said, when they had eaten their supper.

Mrs Owl and three small owlets were soon sound asleep in their home in a hollow tree, but Drew was too worried to sleep.

'There must be someone, somewhere,' he thought, 'who can teach me how to hoot. I must go and see.'

So, in the soft, grey light of early morning, he left the nest and flew on his strong silent wings across the fields to the farmyard. There he saw the farm cat.

'Hello, cat,' called Drew. 'You have eyes which see in the dark like mine. Can you hoot?'

'Meiow, Naow!' grinned the cat.

So Drew peeped into the barn.

'Can you hoot?' he asked Daisy the cow.

'Mooo, noooo!' answered Daisy.

Gilly the Goose stalked across the farmyard.

'Good morning, Gilly,' cried Drew. 'Please, can you hoot?'

'Honk, honk! Bonk, honk! I should think not!' snapped Gilly haughtily.

Brag, the brown dog, sat outside the farmhouse door and howled, 'Ow-wow-wo-ow.'

'That's a fine song,' exclaimed Drew. 'Can you hoot, Brag?'

'No,' growled Brag. 'I'm just telling my master it's time for our early morning walk. Wuff! Here he comes. I'm off!'

'Oh, dear,' sighed Drew. 'No one will teach me to hoot, after all. But, goodness, who is that?'

A splendid bird stood on top of the henhouse. On his head he wore a red comb, like a king's crown. His feathers gleamed like silk and he had the most magnificent curling tail feathers.

'Good morning, SIR,' said Drew, very politely. 'Who are you?'

'Good morning, little owl,' the big bird replied. 'I'm King, the cockerel. And now it is daylight, I must make sure everyone is awake.'

King the cockerel threw back his head and crowed.

'Cock-a-doodle-doo-ooo!'

It was the loudest, most splendid voice little Drew had ever heard.

'Itty ooo!' he hooted admiringly.

King stopped in the middle of another crow and stared at Drew.

'Itty what?' he asked. 'That's a weak and wobbly noise to be making!'

'But it's the best I can do-oo,' sobbed Drew. 'Boo-hoo. I wish I could sing like you-oo.'

'Cheer up,' said King briskly. (He was rather a show-off and loved to be admired, so he rather liked Drew.) 'Cheer up, little owl. I'll teach you how to crow. Watch me, and listen carefully.' King stood on tiptoe, opened his beak wide and crowed, over and over again, until at last Drew understood just how it was done.

'Cock-a-whoodle-whoo!' he crowed, so loudly that he bounced right up in the air. He had to spread his wings so he could land safely on the henhouse roof beside King.

'Not bad. Not bad at all,' King told him. 'Well, it's time you went home, young owl. My word, your mother will be proud of you!'

So Drew flew home and crept into the nest beside Mrs Owl, Hugh, Sue and Pru, to sleep until the moon rose again that night.

Then his family had a surprise!

'Never,' said Mrs Owl, 'never have I heard such a wonderful, musical song. Sing it again, Drew.'

So Drew sang his song again, and has been singing it each night ever since.

If you should wake one night when it is still quite dark and hear 'Cock-a-whoodle-whoooo!'

don't worry. You can curl up and go cosily back to sleep, for it isn't King you can hear, calling that it's time to get up.

No, it's Drew the Owl, hooting his own special cry for you as he goes hunting in the moonlight across fields and woods and gardens. 'Cock-a-whoodle-whoooo!'

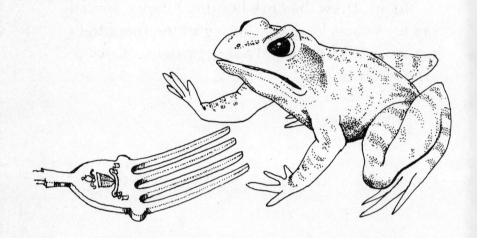

Frizby's royal invitation

Val Annan

Are you sitting comfortably? Then I'll begin.

Mr Noodles owned a shop in the market place. It was full of useful things like yellow buckets, shiny saucepans, black kettles, brown pots and wooden spoons.

One day, a tall green frog hopped into the shop.

'Good-day, Mr Noodles,' said the frog. 'My name is Frizby Frog and I would like a Princess please.'

Mr Noodles stared in amazement at the frog.

'Er . . . I don't stock Princesses, I'm afraid. They are very hard to come by . . .'

'Oh, but the sign above your shop door says 'Anything and everything supplied for the home,' said Frizby stubbornly. 'And I want you to supply me with a Princess!'

'Er . . . what exactly do you want a Princess for?' asked Mr Noodles.

'I want a Princess to kiss me so that I will change into a handsome Prince!' said Frizby. 'You see, I'm too big for the small pond that I live in, but if I marry a Princess I can live in a Palace!'

'But what makes you think *you* will change into a handsome Prince?' asked Mr Noodles.

'Because I've just read a story. It was all about a tall green frog who is kissed by a Princess and the frog then turns into a handsome Prince.'

'But that sort of thing only happens to very special frogs,' said Mr Noodles.

'But I AM a very special frog!' said Frizby indignantly. 'My Mum tells everyone that I'm special!'

'Er . . . perhaps you can come back tomorrow?' said Mr Noodles. 'A Princess might turn up – you never know your luck.'

And indeed a Princess did turn up, just ten

minutes after Frizby Frog had left Mr Noodles' shop! As she went into the butcher's shop next door, Mr Noodles noticed the silver crown on her head. Mr Noodles followed her.

There he found the butcher bowing very humbly. 'Can I interest you in a piece of beef, Your Highness? Or a nice leg of lamb, perhaps?' he said.

The Princess turned up her nose.

'No! No! No! I want something *unusual* to eat. We are *always* having beef or roast lamb!'

'Tripe!' said the butcher. 'Tripe is a most unusual royal dish. Boil it up with some milk and onions and it's fit for a King, Queen or Princess!'

'Oh, very well! I'll try some tripe,' sighed the Princess.

As she was leaving the butcher's, Mr Noodles said nervously: 'Er – s'cuse me, Your Highness . . . but can I interest you in a nice green frog?'

'Can you interest me in a nice green frog!' she said. 'Is he a nice *big* frog?'

'Oh, quite the biggest and tallest frog I've ever seen!' said Mr Noodles.

'Is he young and tender?' asked the Princess.

'Oh, I'm sure he is!' said Mr Noodles.

'Good!' said the Princess. 'Deliver him to the Palace tomorrow for lunch!'

'Oh, yes, Your Highness!' said Mr Noodles.

So, when Frizby Frog turned up the next morning he was delighted when Mr Noodles said, 'I'm to take you to the Palace for lunch!'

'Oh, good!' said Frizby Frog. 'I wonder what we'll have to eat? I've never had a Royal Invitation before!'

So Mr Noodles and Frizby Frog went to the Palace. They rang the silver bell on the silver gates.

'Come round to the kitchen door!' yelled the Princess.

'Well, really!' said Frizby Frog. 'I don't think much of her manners – fancy sending a guest to the kitchen door! I don't think she's a very NICE Princess!'

'Er . . . you didn't ask for a nice one,' said Mr Noodles.

And when the Princess opened the back door, Frizby Frog didn't like the look of her at all. It wasn't that she wasn't beautiful or anything like that but she had a nasty gleam in her eye when she looked at him. She pushed Mr Noodles away before he could introduce Frizby Frog.

'Send your bill through the post!' she said.

And then the rude Princess poked Frizby Frog with a big fork.

'Hmm,' she said. 'There's not much meat on these thin legs of yours.'

'Not much meat! Well, really! I haven't come

31

here to be insulted! I've had enough of this!'

And before the Princess could grab him, Frizby Frog leapt away. He ran after Mr Noodles.

'Oh, Frizby Frog! I think you've had a narrow escape,' said Mr Noodles. 'I do believe the Princess wanted to *eat* you!'

'Eat me!' said Frizby Frog. 'Nonsense! She wanted to kiss me so that I would turn into a handsome Prince and then she could marry me and nag me and push me around with a big fork for the rest of my life! NO THANK YOU! I'm going back to my nice green pond. I rather like being a big frog in a small pond after all!'

The little cat with the very long tail

Diana Webb

Are you sitting comfortably? Then I'll begin.

There was once a toy cat with a small round yellow body and a very very long, very very fat yellow tail. His tail was so long that it reached right to the end of the shelf in the shop where the little cat sat waiting for someone to buy him. All the other animals on the same shelf had to sit behind it.

'I don't know why you need such a long fat tail,' said the toy rabbit who sat next to him. 'It takes up too much room.'

33

'I don't know why you need such long ears,' said the little cat.

'But my ears aren't as long as all that,' said the rabbit. 'Your tail is ten times as long as one of my ears.'

'I can't help it,' said the little cat, who didn't understand why he had such a long tail either, when he could see that all the other cats in the shop had quite short tails. 'Perhaps I shall find out one day why I have such a long fat tail.'

'Maybe people could balance on it like a tightrope in a circus,' suggested a toy elephant.

'Maybe,' said the little cat, but he didn't really like the idea of people walking on his tail.

'Maybe one end of it could be tied to the branch of a tree and people could climb up it like a pole,' said a toy monkey.

'Maybe,' said the little cat, but he didn't really like the idea of people climbing up his tail.

'Maybe people who wanted to cross a river could throw it across the water and use it as a bridge,' said a toy duck.

'Maybe,' said the little cat, but he didn't really like the idea of people using his tail as a bridge. It might get wet.

'Maybe people will just trip over it and get cross,' said the rabbit. 'If you ask me you should have it shortened.'

'No,' said the little cat. 'I don't think I should

do that. I'm sure there must be a good reason why my tail is the way it is.'

Then one day a lady came into the shop. She bought the little cat with the very long tail and she bought the rabbit next to him as well. When she got home she gave the rabbit to her little boy as a present but she took the little cat with the very long tail and put him down by the door to the living room as far away from everyone as she could.

The little cat felt sad.

At night when the little boy was going to bed he dropped his new rabbit by the door. The rabbit laughed at the little cat with the long tail.

'That lady knows now that buying you was a mistake. I expect she's put you by the door to remind her to take you to a jumble sale next time she goes out. But I don't think anyone else would be silly enough to buy something with such a stupid long tail, even at a jumble sale.'

The little cat said nothing, but he was very unhappy.

After the lady had put her little boy to bed she came back into the room and shut the door. She picked up the little cat with the very long tail and sat him at one end of the door. Then she stretched out his tail all along the carpet in front of the bottom of the door. The little cat felt very comfortable with his tail stretched along the bottom of the door. It fitted there very well.

Outside the house the wind was blowing hard. It blew through the gap under the front door into the hall. It blew through the gap under the kitchen door into the kitchen. It blew through the gap under the dining room door into the dining room. It tried to blow through the gap under the living room door into the living room but it couldn't because the little cat's tail was in the way.

The little cat felt the wind pushing against his tail and suddenly he knew why his tail was so long and fat.

'Of course,' he said to himself. 'It's to stop the wind blowing under the door into the room, so the people inside don't catch cold.' And he was extremely happy.

The wind tried very hard to push its way into the room but the little cat's tail was so long and so fat that the wind couldn't get past no matter how hard it blew.

'I always knew I should find out one day why I had such a very special kind of tail' said the little cat. He looked at the rabbit's short stubby tail. 'It's only a very special kind of tail that can keep out something as big and strong as the wind!'

Chick, Chicklet and Chick-a-Ling

Ivy Eastwick

Are you sitting comfortably? Then I'll begin.

'Hurry! hurry!' said Mrs Hen. 'Come along out now. All of you.'

The three little eggs stayed as they were.

Eggs.

Just eggs.

Not a chirp.

Not a cheep.

Just three brown-shelled eggs.

'It's time,' called Mrs Hen. 'It's Spring. Come along out!'

The three little eggs stayed as they were.

Eggs.

Just eggs.

Not a chirp.

Not a cheep.

Just three brown-shelled eggs.

'I have sat here too long. Come on. The sun is shining,' said Mrs Hen.

The three little eggs stayed as they were.

'The sky is blue. Oh, so very blue,' said Mrs Hen. 'Will nothing bring you out?'

The three little eggs stayed as they were.

'The worms are moving around under the ground. They are waiting for you,' said Mrs Hen.

There was a sound from one egg.

Tap.

There was a sound from the second egg.

Tap. Tap.

There was a sound from the third egg.

Tap. Tap. Tap.

'And about time too!' said their mother. A little downy yellow head peeped out of one shell.

'Hello, Mother,' he chirped.

'Hello, Chick,' said his mother.

A second yellow head peeped out of the second shell.

'Hello, Mother,' he chirped.

'Welcome, Chicklet,' said his mother.

38

The third yellow head broke through his shell. He looked all round him. Up. And down.

'Where are the worms?' he asked. 'Where is the blue sky? Where is the sun?'

His mother looked up and down too. The sky was grey. The sun had gone.

'I'm going back,' said the third little chick crossly. 'I'm going back into the shell. There isn't any sun. There isn't any blue sky. And there are no worms!'

He stamped his foot angrily. Then he kicked the eggshell out of the nest.

'You can't go back, Chick-a-Ling,' said his mother. 'The eggshell is broken.'

'I don't care,' said Chick-a-Ling. 'I am going back. And I shall wait there until the worms come up, the sun comes out and the sky turns blue.'

And he stomped back into his eggshell.

'Oh, dear,' said his mother. 'What a tiresome chick this one is. How can I help it if the weather changes and the worms hide?'

It began to rain.

'Come under my wing,' said Mrs Hen. Chick and Chicklet hopped under their mother's wing.

Chick-a-Ling stayed where he was – in the open-topped shell.

'You'll get wet,' said his mother.

'Don't care,' said Chick-a-Ling.

'Please come, Chick-a-Ling,' said Chicklet.

'Do come, Chick-a-Ling,' said Chick.

'NO!' Chick-a-Ling answered. 'I'll wait here, till the sky turns blue and the sun comes out and the worms come up from the ground.'

There was a bright flash of lightning.

'What's that?' asked Chick-a-Ling.

'It's lightning,' said his mother.

'I don't like lightning,' said Chick-a-Ling.

'Then come under my wing and you won't see it,' said his mother.

'NO!' said Chick-a-Ling.

There was a loud crash of thunder.

'What's that?' asked Chick-a-Ling.

'It's thunder,' said his mother.

'I don't like thunder,' said Chick-a-Ling.

'Then come under my wing and you won't hear it,' said his mother.

'No!' said Chick-a-Ling.

'You'll get very wet out there,' said his mother.

'Don't care,' said Chick-a-Ling.

'You'll catch cold,' said his mother.

'Don't care,' said Chick-a-Ling.

Chick and Chicklet were dry and warm under their mother's wing. Soon Chick-a-Ling was drenched. His feathers hung limp. His little feet were cold. His little eyes began to run with water. He shivered.

'Please, Chick-a-Ling, dear little Chick-a-Ling, come under my wing.' his mother pleaded.

But he was stubborn.

'No,' he said.

'Well, then, *I* must come to *you*,' she said, and she walked out of the nest to where Chick-a-Ling stood shivering in his eggshell. She put her wing over him and then she clucked to her other two chicks who came and sheltered under her other wing.

She said: 'You'll soon be dry, Chick-a-Ling.'

Chick-a-Ling shivered under her wing. Then he grew a little warmer and a little drier and his eyes stopped watering and he stopped shivering. 'Mother is right,' he thought. 'It is better here than out there in the rain, with the lightning and the thunder.'

He stayed there for ten minutes. Then he heard his mother call: 'You may come out now, my little ones. The rain has nearly stopped and the sun is out.'

Chick came hopping out.

Chicklet came hopping out.

But Chick-a-Ling said: 'No. I'd rather stay here.'

'Oh, Chick-a-Ling,' said his mother. 'Come out and see how pretty the world can be.'

'No,' said Chick-a-Ling.

He heard Chick and Chicklet talking together. They were saying things like: 'Sweet. Sweet. Pretty-sweet. Pretty-sweet. Cheep-sweet. Sweet-cheep.'

He poked his head out from under his mother's wing.

He looked up at the sky.

It was blue.

He looked up at the sun.

It was golden.

AND there was a beautiful SOMETHING in the sky.

The SOMETHING was shaped like a bow.

A HUGE bow.

It was blue and mauve and pink and green and yellow.

'Mother! Mother! Look!' cried Chick-a-Ling. 'Up there! What is it?'

His mother looked and then she laughed.

'It is the April Rainbow, Chick-a-Ling,' she told him.

'I LIKE rainbow, Mother,' said Chick-a-Ling, and he stepped right out of his shell.

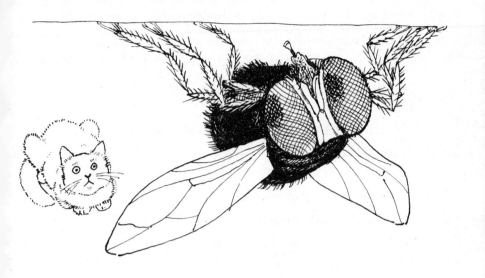

Little fly on the ceiling

Angela Pickering

Are you sitting comfortably? Then I'll begin.

The little fly was walking on the ceiling. From the corner by the door to the corner by the window. From the corner by the window to the corner by the door.

'Little fly, little fly,' yawned the cat on the rug, 'why do you walk on the ceiling?'

The little fly walked across the ceiling to the lampshade. He hung upside down by his sticky feet and looked at the cat on the rug.

43

'Zzzzzz. Why shouldn't I walk on the ceiling if I want to?'

'No reason,' said the cat on the rug, 'no reason at all. I just wondered why, that's all. *Most* of us walk on the ground.'

'Ah,' said the little fly. 'Then most of you can't see the table, Grandpa's table laid ready for tea.'

He walked across the ceiling to the corner by the cupboard. From the corner by the cupboard to the corner by the shelf.

'Little fly, little fly,' yawned the cat on the rug, 'that's not a reason. Grandpa would never invite you for tea. Why, tell me why, do you walk on the ceiling?'

'Zzzzzz. Why shouldn't I walk on the ceiling if I want to?'

'No reason,' said the cat on the rug, 'no reason at all. I just wondered why, that's all. *Most* of us walk on the ground.'

'Ah,' said the little fly, 'then most of you can't see Grandpa's pot plants growing on the sill.'

He walked across the ceiling. From the corner by the shelf to the corner by the cupboard. From the corner by the cupboard to the corner by the shelf.

'Little fly, little fly,' yawned the cat on the rug, 'that's not a reason. Grandpa's plants will grow no matter how high you are. Why, tell me why, do you walk on the ceiling?'

'Zzzzzz. Why shouldn't I walk on the ceiling if I want to?'

'No reason,' said the cat on the rug, 'no reason at all. I just wondered why, that's all. *Most* of us walk on the ground.'

'Ah,' said the little fly, 'then most of you can't see the top of Grandpa's shiny head. Such a smooth bald head it is. No hair left at all. I would like to settle on Grandpa's shiny head.'

'Little fly, little fly,' yawned the cat on the rug, 'that's not a reason. Grandpa would never let you settle on his shiny bald head. Why, tell me why, do you walk on the ceiling?'

'Ah,' said the little fly, 'so many questions. Do you really want to know why I walk on the ceiling?'

'Well,' yawned the cat, 'it's what I keep asking.'

The little fly walked across the ceiling. From the corner by the shelf to the corner by the door. From the corner by the door to the very very middle. Right over the mat where the cat was sitting.

'Zzzzzz,' said the little fly. 'I walk on the ceiling so that Grandpa's cat cannot swot me with his paw. Zzzzzz. That's why!'

45

And then the little fly sang this song:

The Little Fly's Song

I get a kind of feeling
When I'm walking on the ceiling
That the cat is waiting for me down below.
My head is kind of reeling
When I'm walking on the ceiling,
I am better up, and down I will not go.
I would rather not be squealing
On the mat. For on the ceiling
Is the safest place of all I surely know.
I've a squealing kind of feeling,
And a reeling kind of feeling,
And a wheeling kind of feeling,
When I'm walking on the ceiling,
For the cat is waiting for me down below.

Hugo the hippo sings

Rachel Ford

Are you sitting comfortably? Then I'll begin.

Hugo the hippo lived in the jungle. He had no reason to be unhappy, but he was. He was unhappy because he could not sing. Every night without fail, he would dream of being a great opera singer. He would sing at the Albert Hall and everyone would applaud and cheer. He would be dressed in a top hat and tails. He would have a beautiful black velvet bow-tie.

Every morning when Hugo woke up, he would feel so disappointed, because none of it was true. It was just a dream.

One starlit night, just as Hugo was saying his prayers, a very bright star caught his eye. Then he remembered what his mother had told him when he was a baby hippo: 'If you ever see a very bright star shining in the sky you must make a wish, but you must not tell anyone what you have wished for.'

So Hugo closed his eyes tightly and made a wish. And then he fell asleep.

While Hugo slept the star came down and said, 'Hugo dear, your wish shall be granted.'

The next morning when Hugo woke up, he opened his mouth to yawn and the most lovely sound came out of his mouth. He was so happy, he jumped around and laughed. He could sing! He decided he would have a party for all of his friends. He invited Stripes the tiger; Ellie the elephant; his best friend Joshua Mud, the hippo who lived next door; Lilly the lioness and Aunty Antelope.

Hugo had a troublesome time trying to get the party ready because hippos are large animals and tend to be rather clumsy. Once he put his foot in the jelly, slipped, and landed in the cake. But at last everything was ready. He put on his best jungle trousers and his very brightly coloured holiday shirt. Then his guests started to arrive. They were all dressed in their best clothes too.

Lilly the lioness was wearing a very fetching pink frilly skirt. They had a wonderful time.

When they were all sitting around the table, Hugo stood up. In a very loud voice, he said, 'I can sing!'

The animals all looked at one another in amazement.

'Oh, no you can't, Hugo,' they said.

'But I *can*,' replied Hugo, 'and what's more, I will sing to you now.' Hugo started to sing. The animals couldn't believe their ears. Hugo was making the most beautiful sound.

Nearby in the jungle, some people were on a safari. When they heard this wonderful singing they just had to find out what it was. They carefully followed the sound of the music and found themselves at Hugo's home.

They knocked on the door and were rather surprised when it was opened by a lioness in a pink frilly skirt.

'Can I help you?' she asked.

'We are looking for the person who was singing so beautifully just a few minutes ago,' said one of the men.

'Oh, that's Hugo the hippo,' replied Lilly. 'He's over there.'

The men told Hugo of a talent competition that was being held the very next evening at the Albert Hall in London. Hugo was very excited.

They all got on an aeroplane and flew to London straight away, and the next night, Hugo the hippo found himself at the Albert Hall dressed in top hat and tails and wearing a black velvet bow-tie round his neck.

Hugo was the last one to go on stage before the judges decided who was to be the winner of the competition and he sang beautifully!

The judges loved his singing and they gave him full marks. Hugo was the winner! He was presented with a big gold cup full of strawberry jam sandwiches!

At last Hugo's dream had come true, and he was a world-famous opera singer.

The dustbin cat

May K. Randell

Are you sitting comfortably. Then I'll begin.

An enormous striped marmalade cat, who weighed as much as a bag of oranges, sat on the new dustbin lid. The lid shone in the sun. It was nice and warm, so the cat purred happily.

Small Black Dog lived across the road. HE was tied up to a shady tree. He wished he was a marmalade cat who could sit on a warm dustbin lid.

But it was a dustbin-emptying day! And along came the dust-cart. Rattle-clang-BANG!

51

Fred the dustman leapt off the dust-cart. He began to empty all the bins in the road. Small Black Dog didn't like the noise, so he began to bark and all the neighbourhood dogs joined in! There was a terrible din as the dustbins were flung down and lids crashed to the ground. Still the enormous marmalade cat, who weighed as much as a bag of oranges, didn't get off his dustbin lid.

Up came Fred the dustman.

'OFF! OFF YOU GET, ginger cat,' he yelled.

'Miaow-Merrow,' went the dustbin cat loudly, which meant: 'I WON'T!'

Small Black Dog ran down as far as his rope would let him. He laughed and laughed. 'Arf! Arf! Arf!' Fred placed his hands on his hips. He stuck out his jaw and made a terrible face at the marmalade cat.

Then he said very softly, 'If you don't clear off that dustbin lid NOW, I'm going to have to push you off!'

But the cat only sat tight and spread himself all over the dustbin lid. Then he sharpened his claws on the edge of it, which made the dustman howl!

'Yee-ow, Merrow, Mee-ow!' the marmalade cat went, which meant: 'Just you try anything, mate, and see what happens to you . . .'

Small Black Dog was enjoying himself watching. He laughed until tears ran down the end of his little wet black nose.

'Arf! Arf! Arf! Arf! ARF!' he went, and all the other dogs in the neighbourhood, although THEY didn't know what was going on, laughed too!

Then Fred shouted across to his driver: 'Turn off the engine a minute, Joe. We've got us a fat, stubborn, old, ginger cat here, who won't get off this dustbin lid.'

'Why don't you push him off then, Fred?' called the driver.

But when Fred put out a hand, the enormous, striped, marmalade cat, who weighed as much as a bag of oranges, hissed and spat, and then ruffled and fluffed up all his fur. He waved his tail angrily. He got out all his sharpened claws. He was ready for anything!

'YOWL! ROWL! YOWL!' he went, which meant: 'I shall NOT get off this dustbin lid until *I* am ready!'

'You awful old cat!' cried Fred the dustman. 'Don't you know I have *got* to empty this dustbin? Get off that lid before I – '

'BIN! BIN! BIN! BI-IN! Breakfast time!' A nice, kind voice floated up the drive.

'BI-IN! *Please* hurry, Bin!' it called. And the enormous, striped, marmalade cat slid off the shiny dustbin lid and hurried away to get his breakfast.

'Well, I never! What a funny name for a cat! BIN!' said Fred, taking off his cap and mopping his forehead, and he quickly emptied the new dustbin.

Then Small Black Dog went back up his garden to dig up a breakfast bone and the dust-cart drove off up the hill, with a Brrrrrum-brrrm-clang-bang!

And when Bin the marmalade cat had finished his breakfast, he came back again to sit on the dustbin lid. The lid shone in the sun and the dustbin cat purred happily and went to sleep.

Mr Herbert Herbert's holiday

Margery Goulden

Are you sitting comfortably? Then I'll begin.

What's grey, has four legs, a tail and a trunk? No, it's not an elephant. It's a mouse going on holiday. And one mouse in particular. Mr Herbert Herbert. This is what happened.

'I've decided where to go,' said Mr Herbert Herbert, coming out from behind the central heating boiler waving a glossy holiday brochure in his paws.

I was very relieved. He'd been behind the

55

boiler with the brochure so long I'd begun to think I'd never see him again. Not a happy thought when I'd just bought a whole new red cannonball Edam cheese just for him.

'I'm going to Costa del Mouse,' he declared, and immediately began to pack. 'It's time I saw the world.'

'How will you get there?' I asked, pressing a thumb onto the lid of his trunk so that he could lock it. (Like everyone going on holiday, he'd packed too much.) 'Can I give you a lift?'

'No, thank you,' he said. 'I'll just hop on a number nineteen bus.'

And he did.

The house was very quiet without Mr Herbert Herbert, like your house is when you're at playgroup. Lovely, I thought. The whole place to myself! How I'd enjoy it. No squeak in the ear to wake me up an hour sooner than I wanted to wake up. No paw to switch off my favourite television programme so that Mr Herbert Herbert could watch Monster Mouse on the other channel. No demands for 'more Edam cheese' just when I was up to my ears in bubbles in the bath. Nobody to tear my newspaper, nibble my apples, spill my coffee, step on the toothpaste (with the top off) or, worst of all, gallop over the piano keys whenever the mood took him, yelling:

I'm happy when I'm singing,
I'm happy when I dance,
I'm happy happy as can be,
The song and dance mouse, that's me!

Of course, there's a lot more to his song than that. I call it the song without end. And if you've ever heard a mouse sing you'll know just how dreadful it sounds and just how beautifully peaceful the house was without Mr Song and Dance Mouse.

There was quiet and I loved it.

I did. Didn't I?

I must. I had what I wanted. Everything quiet. Everything to myself. My newspaper. My apples. My coffee. The bathroom. The television. The piano. Most especially the piano. But, oh, dear! How quiet the piano suddenly seemed. I don't play. Mr Herbert Herbert is the musical one. And there it stood. Silent.

It was then, looking at the piano, that I realized the truth. I missed Mr Herbert Herbert. I was lonely without him. I didn't want quiet. I didn't want the house, or anything, to myself. I wanted Mr Herbert Herbert back home and I still had another whole week alone. He'd gone to the Costa del Mouse for a fortnight.

I went into the kitchen and sat, very quietly, reading my newspaper and drinking my coffee, wishing Mr Herbert Herbert were there. Then I heard the rattle of the letterbox in the hall. A jolly, sunny, wish-you-were-here postcard from Mr Herbert Herbert no doubt, I thought, miserably. But it wasn't.

I was just in time to see Mr Herbert Herbert's trunk, even fuller than before, thud down onto the hall carpet. It was followed by Mr Herbert Herbert himself, complete with sombrero.

'Hasta la vista!' he said. That's 'goodbye' in Spanish, the language they speak on the Costa del Mouse. He'd meant to say 'hello' of course, but he'd only been there a week so I thought it a very good try. It was nearly right.

'Hello,' I said. 'Back so soon? How was the Costa del Mouse? How was the world?'

'There was no Edam cheese,' he said. 'And no piano.'

'Oh!' I said. 'So that's why you're back so soon.'

'No,' he said, trotting off to the back of the central heating boiler. 'I missed you. Did you miss me?'

I gave him the largest supper of Edam cheese he'd ever had in his life, and then I said, 'Won't you play the piano for me – please, Mr Herbert Herbert? And sing?'

And he did.

Wriggly Worm and the new pet

Eugenie Summerfield

Are you sitting comfortably? Then I'll begin.

One lazy day in June, Wriggly Worm was lying in the long grass enjoying the scent of flowers all round him. Anthea Ant came bustling along.

'Ah, there you are, Wriggly,' she said, 'I've something important to say to you.'

'Yes?' said Wriggly.

Anthea settled down beside him. 'I'm worried about Cirencester,' she began.

'Oh, not again!' groaned Wriggly. Cirencester, the sad stick insect, was a constant problem.

'How can anyone stop him from being sad for very long?'

'Ah-ha!' said Anthea, looking pleased with herself, 'I think I know the answer to that question.'

'You do?' Wriggly was glad to hear this.

'He's sad,' went on Anthea, 'because he needs someone to love him. And someone he can love too.'

'But, Anthea, we're his friends. We love him,' said Wriggly.

'Yes, yes, I know, but it's not the same as having someone or something of his very own.'

Then Wriggly Worm had a wonderful idea. 'What Cirencester needs is a pet,' he said.

Anthea wasn't so sure at first. She had never heard of a stick insect having a pet. She asked Wriggly Worm, 'What kind of a pet should it be, Wriggly? He'll need something quiet and friendly?'

Wriggly Worm went down into his secret tunnel to have a think about this. Then up he came, all excited.

'I've got it, Anthea! Leave it to me. I'll find Cirencester a nice quiet pet he can love.'

Anthea was delighted. 'Thank you, Wriggly. You are wonderful,' she said. 'Now I must go. I've got so much else to do.'

Wriggly Worm knew where there was a lost

pet who would just suit Cirencester. And as soon as Wriggly had found it, he sent it round to Cirencester right away.

So, later on, it was no surprise to Wriggly Worm when a note arrived by pigeon post which said: 'Please come to a special picnic today to meet my new pet. Lots of lettuce for tea. Love Cirencester. P.S. And thank you, Wriggly.'

Everybody had had notes by pigeon post that day. Sloppy Slug, Brown Snail, all the little Brown Snails, and Anthea Ant had all been invited. The little Brown Snails were all smart and shiny, ready for the picnic. Sloppy Slug was looking forward to lettuce for tea. He hoped it wouldn't all be eaten up before he got there. 'I think we'd better hurry,' he said. 'We don't want to be late for tea.'

'Wriggly,' said Brown Snail, as they crawled along together, 'what sort of a pet will it be?'

'Ah! yes, well . . . ' said Wriggly, because he knew. 'You'll have to wait and see.'

All the way along the little Brown Snails played guessing games. They were trying to find out what Cirencester's pet could be.

'It couldn't be an ant or an elephant.'

'It couldn't be a quail or a little Brown Snail.'

'Could it be a squirrel, with a big bushy tail?'

'Tell us, Wriggly. Tell us what it'll be.'

'No, no, no! You wait and see. Whatever it is, it will make Cirencester happy.'

Everyone was pleased about that. So, what a shock they all got when they reached Cirencester's special part of the garden and found him crying.

'Oh, woe, woe is me! Oh, why do sad things always happen to *me*? Oh, woe, oh, woe!'

Wriggly Worm hurried forward.

'Whatever's the matter, Cirencester?' he asked. 'We didn't expect to find you in tears.'

There was Cirencester sitting hunched up on a huge smooth brown stone, sobbing. 'I've lost him! I've lost my new pet,' he cried.

'We'll look for him,' said Wriggly. 'Everybody look for Cirencester's new pet.'

'Yes, yes,' cried all the little Brown Snails. They began to scurry hither and thither.

Then one called out, 'Wriggly, tell us what we're looking for?'

'Well,' Wriggly replied, 'his name's Shy. He's brown and smooth and rather like that huge thing Cirencester's sitting on – ' He stopped suddenly. Then he said, 'Cirencester! You old silly, you're sitting on your new pet tortoise. You haven't lost him at all!'

Cirencester jumped down and hopped round to one end where there was quite a pile of lettuce leaves. A head came out of the shell and said in a whisper, 'Hello, I'm Shy.' And then popped back in again.

'He's very friendly really,' explained Cirencester, 'when he gets used to people.'

And he was. He gave the little Brown Snails rides on his back. He told them tortoise stories they had never heard before. They all had a lovely picnic. Everyone enjoyed it, especially Cirencester.

Nozzle the ant-eater

Christopher Newby

Are you sitting comfortably? Then I'll begin.

Nozzle is an ant-eater who lives in a small town. His cleverest friend is a bright red elephant called Horatio, who spends most of his spare time in the local swimming pool.

One day, when they were talking together, Horatio asked, 'Have you ever caught an ant, Nozzle?'

'No, I've never even thought about it,' replied Nozzle. 'Why do you ask?'

'Well, you are called an ant-eater,' said Horatio,

'but you are so nice I can't really imagine you eating ants.'

And as Horatio spoke, Nozzle suddenly thought: Horatio is right. I am *called* an ant-eater. I ought to be able to catch ants, and I've never even tried. Without saying another word, he left Horatio paddling in the pool and made his way to Hazelnut Wood, to catch his very first ant.

He had been looking for nearly an hour and was getting very fed up by his lack of success, when he heard a little voice.

'Hello, Nozzle,' it called, 'what are you doing?'

To his amazement Nozzle saw that it was his friend Cyril the ant talking.

'Don't move!' shouted Nozzle. 'I'm coming to catch you.'

Cyril looked surprised.

'But Nozzle, it's me! Cyril! your friend!' he exclaimed.

'But *I'm* an *ant-eater*,' announced Nozzle, trying to look fierce.

'You wouldn't eat me!' Cyril laughed. And with that, he ran down a rabbit burrow. Nozzle followed, putting his long nose right into the hole. Cyril carried on running, quite sure that Nozzle was only playing. Nozzle pushed harder, but he could not reach Cyril, who had now run right through the burrow and out to the other side. 'I'm over here, Nozzle,' he teased, enjoying the game more and more. Feeling rather annoyed, Nozzle tried to pull his nose out of the hole. It was then that he realized he was stuck. That made Cyril laugh even more. 'That should teach you not to chase your friends,' he said.

'I'm completely stuck!' said Nozzle. 'Please help me.'

'Well,' said Cyril, suddenly starting to feel sorry for Nozzle, 'I'd like to help, but I'm not strong enough to pull you out by myself. I'll go and look for Horatio the elephant.'

'Please be quick,' said Nozzle.

After only five minutes, Cyril found Horatio paddling in the swimming pool.

'Hello, Horatio,' he called. 'Can you come and help Nozzle please?'

'Of course,' smiled Horatio. 'What's the trouble?'

Cyril told him all about Nozzle's accident. Soon they were both hurrying back to Hazelnut Wood.

'Are you still stuck, Nozzle?' asked Horatio.

'Yes,' whispered Nozzle, who was now feeling rather ashamed of himself for chasing Cyril.

Carefully, Horatio wrapped his trunk around Nozzle's tail, and pulled. Nothing happened.

Horatio pulled again, and this time, his nose moved just a little. One more pull, and 'Pop' – out it came.

'Thank you, Horatio,' said Nozzle quietly, 'and, Cyril, I'm sorry I chased you. I'll never chase an ant again even if I am an ant-eater.'

And that is why, from that day to this, Nozzle has never eaten a single ant. Cyril is now one of his very best friends.

The warthog and the unicorn

Sandra Hannaford

Are you sitting comfortably? Then I'll begin.

Sometimes Warthog wished he had never found out how ugly he was, or that the tiger who had first told him he was had simply eaten him instead. He remembered how Tiger had snarled and swished his tail. 'What a horrid sight!' he had laughed.

'I beg your pardon, sir,' hiccuped Warthog, who had been eating roots. 'What is a horrid sight?'

'You are!' the tiger roared. 'If I were twice as hungry as I am I wouldn't put my smallest tooth in you. You're just too ugly to eat!'

He left Warthog hiccuping, 'You can't mean me! I'm not that ugly. I'm not!'

But he was. He would stand and look at himself in the pool and see his big flat nose and the whiskers on his chin; his warts like currants on a bun and teeth like piano keys; his red eyes squinted inwards and his ears stuck outwards and his belly touched the ground. And he would whisper to himself. 'It's true. I am too ugly to be seen.'

Now the King of the forest in those parts was a magic horse, a unicorn. He was blazing white with silver hooves and a single golden horn.

One day the King came down to the river alone to drink, and halted in surprise. For there on the river bank was a hole; and in the hole was mud; and in the mud was an animal the King had never seen before, making the most appalling din. Deep in the mud it snorted and roared, gulped and splashed, squelched and sucked and slurped. And all the time it sang to itself making noises like a train. The King crept closer to watch.

It was, of course, Warthog in the hole and all at once he opened his eyes and saw the King.

'Oh, hello,' he said, 'Nice day. Hot. Do you

69

want some mud?'

'I beg your pardon?' said the King.

'Some mud.' Warthog thought he should explain. 'This is mud. Wonderful stuff. Cool yer. Fun.' And to show the King what fun it was he stood on his head and lay on his back and surged and sploshed and ducked like a submarine, explaining all the time at the top of his voice until birds took off from the trees a mile downstream.

'Try it yourself!' Warthog cried.

'I don't really think that –' said the King; but just as he spoke, he fell in.

Now a warthog's legs are short and thick, just right for mud; but a unicorn's are long and thin and quite wrong.

The mud got everywhere and Warthog didn't help. When he should have pushed, he pulled; and when he should have pulled, he pushed – very hard, until the King was covered in weeds and mud.

'Like it?' asked Warthog hopefully.

The King spat out some weeds and thought. Then he asked. 'Why do you like mud so much, my friend?'

'Because I can hide in it,' said Warthog. 'And no one can see how ugly I am.' He sighed.

'Does everyone call you ugly?' asked the King.

'They say I'm even too ugly to eat!' Warthog sobbed.

At this very moment out jumped Toad awakened from his sleep by the noise and swollen with rage.

'What! what!' he croaked. 'What do you mean by making that din? You spoil my sleep and spoil the view. I'll see you pay for this, splashing mud everywhere!'

Just then Toad realized there was something very familiar about the second warthog. 'Oh dear,' he squeaked, 'Your Majesty! How could I know it was your royal self?'

'Toad,' said the King, 'you are a snob. It should not have mattered whether you knew or not. Go and fetch all the animals in the forest and bring them here at once.'

So Toad set off more frightened than he had ever been before and soon every creature in the forest stood on the river bank before a King they had never seen so plastered with mud and hung with weed. And he looked very grim indeed.

'Now listen to me,' said the King. 'This is Warthog. You all frightened him so much by calling him a horrid sight, that he decided to live here in this hole covered with mud where none of you would see what you call his ugliness. Stand up, Warthog!'

'I am standing up, Your Majesty,' said Warthog,

deep in the mud and holding up the King.

'Very well,' said the King. 'Now, you animals, why do you call this good warthog an ugly beast? You, Rat, you tell me.'

'Well – ' said Rat, twitching his tail, and looking embarrassed.

'You, Tiger,' said the King, 'you tell me.'

'Aaaah, Your Majesty.' The tiger showed his teeth but couldn't say anything.

'He's different,' said Toad, very loudly, and wished at once he had not.

'Different?' asked the King. 'Different, Toad? You all are different, every one of you. If being different means being ugly then all of us are ugly too. Stand up, Warthog!' said the King again.

'I AM standing up, your Highnessty,' Warthog groaned, still not very sure of what was going on.

The King frowned terribly in case anyone should laugh. 'You have all been snobs,' he told the animals. 'You left poor Warthog here alone and let him cover himself with mud because he is different from you all. And here I found him, an animal more honest, kind and gentle than any one of you. Henceforth,' said the King, 'Warthog will live at Court. He will take his place – '

'Your Majesty!' Warthog tried to interrupt.

' – in every procession,' continued the King.

'Your Majesty,' Warthog tried again, 'I'd rather stay here, if you please.'

'But why?' asked the King.

'Because of the mud,' Warthog explained. 'And this hole of mine, you see, is home.'

'I see,' said the King. 'Then this is my command. All of you here will come every day to Warthog's hole to talk to him.'

And so from that day onwards Warthog never lacked for friends and no one ever told him he was ugly again. And the King came once a week as well, to try the mud (or so he said), and to talk with his good friend.

Just a bad day

Rosalie Eisenstein

Are you sitting comfortably? Then I'll begin.

Badger woke up early. For some reason he just did not feel right. He did not want to get up, yet he did not feel like sleeping either. He humped and bumped around under the covers. Every so often he heaved enormous sighs. At last he decided to get up.

He made breakfast and sat munching toast and strawberry jam. He had received the jam as a present, the day before. He had looked forward to breakfast so he could taste it. It was quite delicious but he did not enjoy it.

Hoggy arrived not long afterwards.

'Are you ready?' he asked.

'Ready for what?' said Badger rudely.

'I thought we had decided to take a walk this morning,' said Hoggy.

'Oh, I'm not in the mood,' said Badger. 'In fact I am in a thoroughly bad mood today,' he added.

'Perhaps you are ill,' said Hoggy. 'You don't look ill though. In fact you look quite well. Yes, you look very well,' he continued, 'except you do look cross. Perhaps you are ill after all.'

'I am not ill,' shouted Badger, 'and I feel just fine. It's just a bad day.'

'Come for a walk anyway,' persuaded Hoggy. 'I am sure it will make you feel better.'

'Oh, all right,' grumbled Badger.

All through the walk he dragged along behind Hoggy. Whatever Hoggy said, Badger just grunted in reply, and he grumbled continually.

'I am tired.'

'I am hungry.'

'Oh, it is a bad day.'

He almost tripped over a tortoise who was crossing the path in front of him.

'Mind where you are going!' shouted Badger.

'I am terribly sorry,' said the tortoise.

'And so you should be,' replied Badger.

Hoggy was very surprised at Badger. 'He is in a bad mood,' he said to himself. 'Come back to my house,' he said to Badger. 'We will have tea. I baked a cake.'

Badger usually cheered up at the thought of tea but he continued grumbling as he followed Hoggy.

When they had sat down, Hoggy poured tea and put on a plate a round, golden cake. It smelt delicious.

'I only like chocolate cake,' complained Badger, helping himself to a slice. In all, he took three slices, so it must have been nice, but still looked decidedly cross.

They started doing a jigsaw together but Badger soon stood up and stretched. 'I don't feel like doing this jigsaw,' he said. 'Goodbye, I am going home.'

He went straight to bed when he got home, still in a very bad mood.

He awoke next morning feeling his usual self. He ran round to Hoggy's house clutching his jar of strawberry jam.

'I am sorry I was so cross yesterday, Hoggy,' he said. 'It was just a bad day.'

The secret

Kathleen Pateman

Are you sitting comfortably? Then I'll begin.

Richard loved going next door to see Miss Tippit because she had Henry. Henry was a big green parrot, in a shiny cage, who squealed and squawked all the day long. Richard couldn't understand a word it said, but Miss Tippit didn't seem to mind. She talked to Henry from morning till night-time, but still Henry only squawked back.

One day Richard was standing beside Henry's

cage, listening to him squealing, 'Waaak, waaaak, waaaaak!' and not understanding a word he was saying.

'I do wish you would talk properly,' he said, as he watched Henry clean the feathers under his wings. 'All you can say is 'Squawk, squawk.' Then Richard said to him in a very firm voice, 'Why don't you answer me, Henry, when I speak to you?'

Henry stopped scratching himself, and looked at Richard with his head on one side. Then suddenly he said, as plainly as you or I could have done, 'Why can't you fly?'

Richard just stared. He opened his mouth to answer, but Henry interrupted and said again, 'Why can't you fly, Richard Watts?'

Richard was more amazed than ever. 'He even knows my name' he thought, but he answered quickly, 'Because I haven't any wings, silly.'

'Well, I'm cleverer than you, then,' said Henry, ''Cos I can fly *and* talk. I am a very clever parrot. In fact, I must be the cleverest parrot in the whole world.' And he squealed and squawked with delight and scrambled up and down his cage and puffed out all his green and red feathers. Then after a minute or two, he said quite quietly, 'I can sing too. Can you sing?'

'I can a bit,' said Richard.

'Do you know "Polly Put the Kettle On"? Henry asked.

'Yes, we sing that at school,' answered Richard.

'Shall we sing it together, then?' asked Henry, and he climbed down the side of his cage until he was quite close to Richard and together they sang 'Polly Put the Kettle On' right the way through.

'You have a very fine voice,' said Richard, when they had finished.

'I can recite too,' said Henry, and he recited 'I love little pussy, her coat is so warm,' without making a single mistake.

'That was very good,' said Richard. 'What else can you do?'

But Henry just looked hard at Richard, went to the topmost perch in his cage and went straight off to sleep.

Just at that moment Miss Tippit came into the room with a biscuit and a glass of orange juice for Richard.

'Been talking to my Henry, have you?' she said. 'He squawks all day long, but you can never understand a word he says.'

Henry, hearing this, opened one eye and winked at Richard and Richard winked back at Henry.

It was their secret, you see.

Well, you can't tell grown-ups everything, can you?

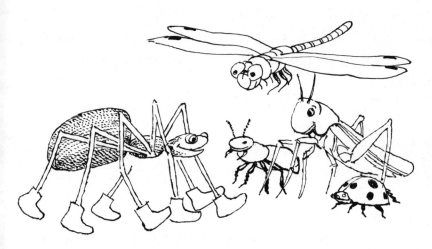

Ary the spider

Irene Holness

Are you sitting comfortably? Then I'll begin.

'Bump! Ouch! Bother! Ow!'

Ary Spider had fallen over. Again. But she mustn't be late today. She hadn't tripped over the broken twigs lying on the garden. She hadn't tripped over the long dry spikes of summer grass. She hadn't even tripped over the little nets of spiderweb her tiny cousins had woven on the lawn. No. Ary had tripped over her own feet. But she must not be late today.

There were a lot of feet to trip over too,

because Ary had a lot of legs. Eight legs. And it does not matter how quickly you count them, eight is a lot of legs and almost too many feet. Ary was always tripping over her own feet.

Ary carefully sorted out her legs again because she simply could not be late on this special day.

'One, two, three, four –
That's half of them.
And now four more –
One, two, three, four.'

Right. Now Ary was all untangled and tidy again.

'Now I must hurry,' she said, 'because today is a very special day and I really must not be late.'

She bustled along busily for a bit, scampering over stones, traipsing over twigs, running over the rockery and gallumping over the grass. Then she came to the smooth concrete path.

'Today is tremendously special,' she said to herself, 'and I must not be late. In fact I must be early.'

'Come on, eight legs, keep busy and whirling.'

Over the path she went at a great speed. Then it happened again.

'Bump! Ouch! Bother! Ow!'

Ary tripped over her own feet again and sat, all in a tangle, her legs all anyways whichways, on the path, feeling rather sad and sulky.

'It simply is not funny,

When one is in a hurry,

To have eight legs all tangled.

It keeps one's nerves quite jangled!'

She was speaking to Dotty the Ladybird who was passing on her way to somewhere very special.

'Never mind, Ary. Come along. You must not be late today, you know!'

'Yes, I know,' sighed Ary and sorted out her feet into order again.

'One, two, three, four,

Two behind and two before.

Now let me see – how many more?

One, two, three, four.'

She trundled on, along the garden path and over the garden path and past the birds' high concrete bath. Then, with a tangle of legs and a rush – under the flowery pink rose bush.

'Ary Spider, you are late!' chirruped Greg Grasshopper.

'You made us wait and wait and wait!' squeaked Bertie Beetle.

'But we won't scold you, not today!' smiled Dotty Ladybird.

'It's Ary's birthday! Hip, hooray!' piped up the butterflies, the dragon flies, the bumble bees and all Ary's friends who had gathered under the pink rose bush for her birthday party.

'Presents first,' said Bella Butterfly, and gave Ary a parcel tied up in a rose petal. Ary opened the parcel.

'Oh,' said Ary, in a very little voice (even for a spider), 'a pair of green shoes – just what I wanted.' But she couldn't help wondering what use were two shoes to a person with eight feet.

Then Bertie Beetle gave her a parcel. Ary opened it and inside was a pair of yellow shoes. 'Oh,' she said, 'just what I wanted.' But she couldn't help wondering what use were four shoes to a person with eight feet.

The next present was a pair of red shoes from Dotty Ladybird. 'I did need a pair of red shoes,' said Ary politely. Now she had six shoes – but she still had eight feet.

Delia Dragonfly's parcel was next. Inside was a pair of beautiful blue shoes.

'Ooo!' said Ary, 'I really truly did need a pair of blue shoes.' For now she had eight shoes for her eight feet.

'Put them on, Ary,' shouted all her friends. 'Green ones in front, then the yellow ones, then the red ones, and then the blue ones!'

So Ary put them on and very fine they looked.

'Now for some marching practice,' said Bertie Beetle.

'Attention! Green shoes! Quick march! Green, yellow, red, blue. Green, yellow, red, blue.'

'This is wonderful!' cried Ary. 'I know just which foot to put forward next. I'll never fall over my own feet again!'

And all her friends cheered and followed Ary as she marched happily down the long garden path.

Basil Brown, the fat cat

Richard Coughlin

Are you sitting comfortably? Then I'll begin.

Basil Brown was a ginger and white tom cat and he was fat. He was *much* too fat. His tummy swelled out at each side as if he'd swallowed a football. He was so fat, he could hardly move. People would point at him in the street and laugh at him and say: 'Ha! Ha! Look at that cat! How fat he is! He looks like a jelly on legs!'

Mrs Brown, Basil's owner, could not understand why he was so fat; she only ever gave him *enough* food, never too much.

'I'd better take him to the vet,' she said. 'Perhaps he's ill.'

Mrs Brown had a big cardboard box that she had brought her groceries home from the shops in, and into this box, she put the fat cat Basil and off to the vet they went.

'Hmmm,' said the vet, 'he *is* a fat cat, isn't he? Much too fat.'

'I can't understand it,' said Mrs Brown. 'I only ever give him just *enough* food, never too much.'

'Hmmm,' said the vet again. He examined Basil the fat cat carefully, prodding him here and there with his finger.

'Well,' he said at last, 'he's certainly not ill. I'm afraid there's nothing I can do. I just can't imagine why he is so fat.'

'Oh, well,' said Mrs Brown, and took Basil the fat cat home.

What could it be that made Basil Brown the fat cat so fat? It wasn't that Mrs Brown gave him too much food; she only ever gave him just *enough* food, never too much. It wasn't that he was ill; the vet had said that he certainly wasn't ill. Perhaps Basil the fat cat caught a lot of mice? No, that wasn't the reason he was so fat either; he was much too fat and slow to run after mice. What could the reason be, then? Why was Basil Brown the fat cat so fat?

This was Basil's secret: every night when it was dark and there was nobody about, he went quietly up and down the street where he lived, scavenging food from dustbins. There were a hundred houses on the street where Basil Brown the fat cat lived and that meant that there were a hundred dustbins. And in each one there were lots of good things for a cat to eat; things that people had thrown away. Things like pieces of fish, scraps of meat, chicken legs, even jam sandwiches and sometimes, Basil's favourite, chocolate sponge. It was a banquet fit for a king; and fit for a cat like Basil. So that was Basil the fat cat's secret and that's why he was so fat.

One night when the moon was shining brightly, Basil Brown the fat cat set out to see what he could find. He began with the dustbin belonging to the first house on the street. Standing on his hind legs he pushed the dustbin lid off with his nose. Then he heaved and puffed and panted and pulled his fat body into the bin.

'Ooh, look at all *this*!' he purred happily to himself for there, among the potato peelings and the soggy messy tea-leaves and all the messy, smelly stuff to be found in a dustbin, were four fishes' heads and a pickled onion.

'I can't understand why people throw such lovely food away,' purred Basil the fat cat, chewing and chomping greedily. 'I can't understand it at all, but I'm so glad that they *do* throw it away. Yummy *Yum*.'

When Basil Brown the fat cat had eaten all the fishes' heads and even the pickled onion in Number One's dustbin, he knocked the lid off the dustbin outside Number Two. Then he heaved and puffed and panted and pulled his fat body into the bin.

'Oh, look at all *this*,' he purred happily to himself. There, among the potato peelings and the soggy messy tea-leaves and all the messy, smelly stuff to be found in a dustbin, were six mouldy old sausages, half a corned beef sandwich and a doughnut.

'I can't understand why people throw such lovely food away,' purred Basil the fat cat, chewing and chomping greedily. 'I can't understand it at all, but I'm so glad that they *do* throw it away. Yummy yum.'

When Basil Brown the fat cat had eaten the six mouldy old sausages, the corned beef sandwich and the doughnut in Number Two's dustbin, he knocked off the lid of the dustbin outside Number Three. Then he heaved and puffed and panted and pulled his fat body into the bin.

'Ooh, look at all this!' he purred happily to himself. There, among the potato peelings and the soggy messy tea-leaves and the messy, smelly stuff to be found in a dustbin, were a piece of steak and kidney pie, a half eaten beefburger and an eccles cake with teeth marks on it.

'I can't understand why people throw such lovely food away,' purred Basil the fat cat, chewing and chomping greedily. 'I can't understand it at all, but I'm so glad that they *do* throw it away. Yummy yum.'

In and out of all the dustbins on the street went Basil Brown, the fat cat. In each bin, he found something good to eat and all the time he was getting fatter and fatter. At last, there was only one dustbin left; the one outside Number Ninety-nine, the house where Basil the fat cat lived.

'Mrs Brown's next,' said Basil the fat cat to himself. 'Mrs Brown's dustbin is my favourite. She nearly always throws away some of her delicious home-made chocolate sponge – just what I need to round off a jolly good night's hunting.'

Basil Brown the fat cat knocked the lid off Mrs Brown's dustbin. Then he puffed and panted and pulled his fat body into the bin.

'Ooh, look at all this!' he purred happily to himself. There, among the potato peelings and the soggy messy tea-leaves and all the messy, smelly stuff to be found in a dustbin, was a big slice of home-made chocolate sponge with a huge splodge of raspberry jam inside.

'I can't understand why people throw such

lovely food away,' purred Basil the fat cat, chewing and chomping greedily. 'I can't understand it at all, but I'm so glad that they *do* throw it away. Yummy yum.'

Basil Brown the fat cat was happy. He'd had a good night's eating and the chocolate sponge was scrumptious. But then something terrible happened. Mrs Brown came out of her house to put the empty milk bottles out and saw the lid of her dustbin lying on the ground. 'That's funny,' she said to herself. 'I'm sure I put that lid on before. Perhaps the wind blew it off.' Then she put the lid back on the bin very tightly indeed, so that it would not blow off again. She didn't know that Basil the fat cat was inside the bin.

Basil didn't notice that the lid had been put back on until he tried to get out. No matter how hard he tried, he could not get the lid off. When he realized what had happened, he became very frightened.

'Oh, help!' he wailed. 'Oh, help! Oh, please let me out! Oh, help me! Oh, please let me out!' But nobody could hear him. Basil Brown the fat cat had to stay in Mrs Brown's dustbin all night in the dark, among the potato peelings and the soggy messy tea-leaves and all the messy, smelly stuff to be found in a dustbin.

In the morning, some men came to empty all the bins in the street. A man called Bill lifted up

Mrs Brown's bin, with Basil inside it, and carried it to the big lorry to empty it.

'Crumbs,' said Bill, as he picked the bin up. 'This is a heavy one.' He took the lid off the bin and out jumped Basil Brown the fat cat with a frightened miaow and off he ran away down the street. Of course he couldn't run very quickly because he was so fat, but he ran faster than he had done for a long time.

'What a fat cat,' said Bill the dustbin man.

From that time on, Basil Brown never again went searching for food in dustbins and soon he became quite slim and handsome.

'That's because I only ever give him just *enough* food, never too much,' said Mrs Brown. But Basil Brown just smiled to himself.

The sheep who didn't count

Irene Holness

Are you sitting comfortably? Then I'll begin.

Cedric didn't count. Lambs often don't count and Cedric knew he didn't because everyone was always telling him so. He was one of twin lambs. The small one. The big one was Cecil. Cecil was superior. He counted. Sam the shepherd said so. Every evening when Sam and sheep dog Shap rounded up the flock on the hill and brought them down to the home field, Sam counted them: 'Snowy – one, Sandy – two, Sooty – three, Sally – four, Cecil – five, Cedric – oh, you're too

93

little to count, Cindy – six . . .' and so on and so on, every single day. So Cedric knew he didn't count. He wasn't important at all.

Sometimes teachers from town schools brought their children to see the farm. The children liked all the animals but the smallest ones loved the sheep best because they were smaller than the cows and quieter than the pigs and didn't run away like the hens and their chicks. They were soft and warm and friendly to pat. They were easy to count.

One day Derek came to the farm with his class. Derek was new. He'd only just started school and he couldn't count very well yet.

He practised counting the sheep, giving each one a little pat.

'One, two, three, four – ' Then he saw Cedric. 'Oh, you're just a little one. I like you.' Derek patted Cedric and forgot all about counting.

Oh, dear, thought Cedric, small sheep are never counted.

Just then, a man arrived with a camera slung over his shoulder.

'Hello,' he said to the teacher. 'I'm from the *Meretown News*. I'd like some photographs of the children with the sheep for my paper, please.'

So the children lined up, the tallest at the back, shortest at the front, and some of the sheep lined up with them. The reporter took two pictures. Then he photographed some of the children patting the sheep.

'Right,' he said, 'I need one more picture. Let's have the three smallest children patting a sheep.'

'Good idea,' said the teacher. 'We'll have Angela, Barry and Derek.'

'Oh, but that won't do!' grumbled the reporter. 'I can't see the children properly. That big sheep takes up all the picture.'

Then Derek said, 'There is one little sheep in the flock.'

Cedric thought, Why, that's me! and skipped forward.

'Fine!' said the reporter. 'We need a sheep the same size as the children. That's what counts.'

So Cedric's picture was in the *Mereworth News*, with his name underneath.

'He's little,' everyone said, 'but he's nice, and that's what counts.'

Whenever schoolchildren visited the farm after that, they always looked out specially for Cedric. And Sam the shepherd always counted Cedric first: 'You're everyone's friend, Cedric,' he said. 'You really count now.'